This time it wasn't my fault. It wasn't Nick's fault, and it wasn't even Jake's fault. I don't know whose fault it could be, but our best friend, Jake, is now a vampire. Jake's dad called my dad to let us know that Jake was bitten on the neck by a bat.

A vampire bat.

I'm sure.

My dad told me.

OH NO, OUR BEST FRIEND IS A VAMPIRE

LANCE ZARIMBA

Featherweight Press
www.featherweightpublishing.com

Published by
Featherweight Press
3052 Gaines Waterport Rd.
Albion, NY 14411

Visit Featherweight Press on the Internet:
www.featherweightpublishing.com

Cover Design by Deana Jamroz
Cover art by Dan Skinner
Editing by Lindsay Ketchen

ISBN# 978-1-60820-222-5

Issued 2010

Author's Note

I always thought that writing a book was the hard part. Ha. That was the easy part. The hard parts are the edits and the rewrites and the self doubt. So many people have helped me bring this dream to life. First, I want to thank my nephew Matthew Zarimba, who helped me come up with the idea for this series. Then I would like to thank Georgia Totten, Thea Miller Ryan, Nancy Steedle and Amy Holm (Writer's Without A Clause) for their critique on the first draft of this book. Next comes Laura Baumbach for her faith in my writing, Lindsay Ketchen for her editing help, and Deanna Jamroz and Dan Skinner for the wonderful cover. Pat Dennis and Marilyn Victor for being the sounding board I need and the best traveling companions anyone could have. Dennis Peterson, Paul McKenzie, and Ripley for all their support at home. Grandpa, Grandma, and Riley, I miss you. And thanks to my family (Mom and Jim, Dad and Cheryl, Lorrie, Heather and Joel, Trent and Jess, Aidan and Jacob) for suffering with all my tall tales growing up. Aren't you glad I scared the heck out of you?

Thank you all and so many more...

Lance

It all started right after I thought I had turned my best friend, Nick, into a Zombie, but that's another story. Our friend, Jake, who lives on the other side of town, needed to ride the bus to and from school. Nick and I lived close enough to our school that we usually walked. We're neighbors, living in mirror opposite homes.

Nick sat next to me on our couch trying to listen in on my phone call to Jake. We needed to find out if what Dad had said was really true and see if our best friend was really a vampire.

"Matthew," Jake said, into the phone, "I stepped off the bus and was walking home, minding my own business. As I passed the old cemetery, a bat swooped down out of the trees and bit me on the neck! It wasn't even midnight."

I gasped as I remembered seeing a similar scene in an old Dracula movie.

Jake continued his story. "I reached up and pulled it away from my throat. Its leathery wings flapped in my hand, and I let it go. The bat flew away. I wish I had known that the doctor needed it to see if it had rabies. I would have tried to hang onto it."

"Rabies?" I said.

"The doctor needs to check the bat to see if it has rabies. If we don't find it, I'll have to get a bunch of shots in my stomach to prevent rabies." He paused. "You remember when we saw that movie about the dog that had rabies?" Jake asked.

Two movies came to mind. One my family watched on movie night, and the other one I watched at a sleepover at Nick's. We weren't supposed to have seen that one, but I'm not telling anyone about that, especially Mom.

Images of those bats biting that dog's nose flooded my mind, and I felt bad for Jake.

"Anyway, my parents rushed me to the hospital, and I got one rabies shot already. And now, I'll have to get like a million more shots in my stomach to make sure I don't get rabies."

"Jake," his mother said, "that's not what the doctor said. You only need three more."

"If only I could find that bat that bit me, then I could get out of the rest of the shots."

Nick moved closer to me on the couch. He pressed his ear to the other side of phone. "Turn up the volume. I can't hear him," he said.

I turned the earpiece away from my ear and aimed it in Nick's direction.

"Better," he said.

"Yes, Nick, I'm better," Jake said.

"We can come over after school tomorrow to see you," I said, "and don't forget we have class pictures tomorrow."

"Oh, great. I'll look like a dweeb with this big bandage stuck on my neck. Oh, well. Thanks Matthew, having you guys over will be great. I could use the company." He lowered his voice. "My parents are watching me all the time. They're treating me like a baby, but all the new DVDs and comic books are great."

I could see Jake sitting in the living room with the phone pressed to his head and his hand covering the mouthpiece. His parents were probably sitting in their armchairs, leaning forward, waiting and watching his every move.

"They're driving me crazy. They act like I'm going to grow another head or something," Jake said. "But, I do have a big surprise to show you when you come over."

Nick grabbed the phone from my hand and held it close to his chest so that he could speak to me without Jake hearing.

"Sprouting fangs and turning into a vampire," he whispered.

I grabbed the phone back from him and asked, "Is there anything you'd like us to bring?"

There was a silence as he thought.

Nick extended his neck, pointed to it, and made a biting motion.

I laughed.

Nick laughed.

And Jake laughed. He must have heard us laughing, but his laugh was an evil laugh.

A laugh just like the one mad scientists used in scary movies.

"Why don't you guys bring over a movie for us to watch? Something I could really sink my teeth into..."

CHAPTER TWO

"Dad, what are rabies?" I asked, after I finished brushing my teeth.

Dad scratched his head. "Your mom is a nurse, she would be better able to explain…" his voice trailed off.

My face must have looked disappointed, because he said, "Hang on," and left the bathroom doorway. He returned to my bedroom a few minutes later with an encyclopedia with a "R" on the spine.

Chief, my sheltie, and I were curled under the blankets. His ears flipped up as Dad moved closer with the book.

He flipped through a few pages and finally found something.

"Rabies is a viral infection of the central nervous system of a variety of animals. It is transmitted to man by the bite or lick from the salvia of a rabid dog, cat, wolf, fox, or bat. Symptoms involve fever, restlessness, extreme excitability, severe thirst, and drooling, and it usually results in dea…" Dad stopped reading and closed the book. "I think it's past your bedtime."

"Do you think Jake will be okay?"

"It's too bad that they didn't find the bat that bit him. It would make all the rabies concerns so much easier." Dad rubbed my head, messing up my hair, and turned off the light. "Night."

I waited for an hour and slipped out of bed. "Chief, you stay here and keep the bed warm."

Chief set his head back down on my pillow and let out

a big sigh.

"I'll be right back." Making my way to the study, my flashlight's beam played across the bookshelf and stopped on the encyclopedias. A golden letter "V" glowed on the spine of one book.

The computer would be easier, but I didn't think I could boot it up and go online without alerting my dad. "I know I couldn't sleep until I read this, and Dad just wouldn't understand," I said to myself.

I found what I was looking for: VAMPIRE.

"Once a vampire bat finds its prey, it will return night after night to the same animal to feed on. It is able to find the same cow in a whole herd."

Something moved by the door.

I swung around, almost dropping the book. My flashlight's beam made green eyes glow in the dark. "Chief, what are you doing here?"

His nails clicked on the floor as he slowly approached. His cold wet nose touched my arm. It sent a shiver over my body.

"One more thing," I told him. I pulled out the "R" book and flipped to the page Dad had read. Then I saw the word he had started to read, but stopped. "Usually results in death."

The next morning, Jake was first in line for school pictures. Mrs. Hubers stood in front of him with a comb ready to catch any wild hair and tame it back into place. A huge white bandage was taped to his neck.

"Why do I have to have my picture taken? I'm going to look like a dork," Jake said.

"Jake, you know how much I hate that word," Mrs. Hubers said.

"Even though he is a dork," Little Cody Johnson said. His short stubby body waited at the end of the line.

Mrs. Hubers walked to the end of the line. As she spoke with Little Cody, the photographer returned and handed Jake a dry erase board with Mrs. Hubers name written on it. "Can you hold this sign up so we'll know which class these pictures go to?" he said.

Jake took the sign and sat on the stool.

"I'll take one with you holding the sign and then, we'll take one of you without it. Did you want to remove that bandage before I take your picture?"

"I can't, the doctor won't let me," Jake said.

"He's turning into a vampire," Little Cody shouted.

Mrs. Hubers turned on her heels and walked back to him.

My face flushed red as Nick poked me in the back. "I have an idea to help Jake; we'll talk about it at lunch."

A flash of light blinded us, and we looked at Jake. He looked stunned by the light.

The photographer took the dry erase board back and quickly snapped Jake's picture. He set the board back on the stool as Jake walked back to class. "I need to adjust my camera, hang on one second," he said to me.

"Sure," I said and watched him fiddle with the dials and buttons.

He aimed his camera at the stool and smiled. "Ready. You can set that board on the floor and take a seat."

I walked up and placed it on the floor and sat down. Mrs. Hubers was still scolding Little Cody, so I hoped my hair was in place.

A flash and it was over. I stepped down and it was Nick's turn.

I walked back to our classroom. As I neared the door, Jake had his face in the water fountain. "Man, am I thirsty," he said and stuck his face back into the stream of water.

I stopped dead in my tracks. Thirsty! He was thirsty.

"I don't know why I'm so hot," he said.

Nick ran to join us and bumped into Jake to stop himself. "Jake, you're burning up. Are you on fire?"

I swallowed hard. Weren't thirst and fever two of the signs of rabies, or were they signs of turning into a vampire?

CHAPTER THREE

Lunch time finally came. Jake and Nick found a table as I tried to unlock my locker. It was holding my lunch hostage. As I neared the table I heard Nick and Jake talking about the bat.

"It's too bad I didn't hang onto the bat, it would've saved me so many problems, but I didn't know."

"I would've freaked out if a bat landed on me, let alone bit me," Nick said.

Sitting down, I added, "They say bats can find the same cow that they feed on the night before."

"What are you saying?" Jake asked.

Nick smiled. "Matthew wants to use you as bait at midnight and see what feeds on you. Maybe we can capture the bat that bit you and then you won't have to go through all those shots."

"I did not. Nick, you're making that up." We turned to Jake laughing and stopped.

Jake's eyes started to water. Tears rolled down his cheeks. He wiped them away with the back of his hand and sniffled a few times to clear his nose.

"Are you okay?" I asked. I had never seen Jake cry, so this was a surprise to see.

"I'm fine," he squinted at me. "I don't know why but my eyes hurt. It seems like the light is too bright or something. It's burning my eyes, and they just keep watering."

Nick looked at me and I knew what he was thinking:

SUNLIGHT. Was Jake going to burst into flames and turn into a pile of dust and ashes on the cafeteria's floor?

Jake stopped rubbing his eyes. He opened them and looked at me. They were red.

Blood red.

My breath sucked in suddenly. His bloodshot eyes looked at me, just like in the movies.

He turned to Nick, who gasped also.

Jake turned to me. "What's up? You guys look like you've seen a ghost."

"Not quite," Nick said, under his breath.

"What?" Jake demanded.

Nick looked at me, and his eyes widened.

"Maybe you rubbed your eyes too hard," I offered. "Are your eyes itchy? That's one thing..."

"That vampire's have," Little Cody said. "It's from all the dust in their coffins. Dust makes me cough-in too. Get it?" He coughed a few times and brought one of his arms up to his face. He peeked over his arm. "I vant to bite your neck." He lowered his arm and clicked his teeth together.

"Hi, Mrs. Hubers, how are you today?" Nick said, looking behind Cody.

Little Cody stood up straight and ran out the cafeteria door without looking back.

We laughed as he disappeared through the door. "I knew that would get rid of him," Nick said.

When we stopped, Jake picked up his lunch tray. "I'm going to go to the nurse's office and see what she says." And he left too.

"I wonder what's wrong with Jake, "I said. "You don't think that he's..."

Nick pursed his lips and shook his head. "I'm not sure what to think. I didn't know we had vampire bats around here."

"Neither did I."

Nick leaned forward. "Well, that settles it. We need to help him, and I know just what to do."

I sat up straight in my chair and cringed as he spoke the next words.

"We have to bring Jake to the cemetery tonight to see if that vampire bat comes back to feed on him. Then we'll know for sure if he's turning into a vampire."

CHapter Four

Jake never returned from the nurse's office.

His desk sat empty all afternoon. Mrs. Hubers called me to her desk just before the bell rang. "Are you going to see Jake tonight or over the weekend?"

"I'm not sure. We had plans but with him being sent home..."

"Could you bring Jake his books and homework? Since it's Friday, he'll have them for the weekend."

"Sure," I said. I headed back to my desk, but turned back and asked, "Mrs. Hubers is there something wrong with Jake?"

She sat back in her chair as concern came across her face. "I hope not, but I'm not sure, Matthew. I'm not sure."

"I can drop you off a few blocks away. Is that okay?" Ryan asked. "If I wasn't running late, I'd take you all the way to Jake's house."

Even though my big brother was a few years older than me, he still was nice to me sometimes, well most of the time. He just was moody and liked to be by himself.

"We know," Nick said. "I'm just glad you got us this close."

Ryan pulled over to the curb. "Call if you need a ride back."

"Thanks for the lift," I said. "But Dad said that he'd pick us up, so you don't have to worry about us."

"It's no problem. What are brothers for?" He raised one of his hands off the steering wheel and pointed at me.

I smiled.

"Maybe I should take that back," Ryan said.

"Don't worry; I won't take advantage of your taxi service."

Ryan nodded to the right. "I could drop you off, if you wanted."

I opened the door. "There's a short cut through here. We'll be fine." I grabbed Jake's backpack, which he had left at school, and stepped out of the car.

Nick followed close behind and slammed the door shut.

We waved at Ryan as he drove away.

I started down the sidewalk, when Nick stopped me. "Where are you going?"

"To Jake's." I pointed down the block.

"The shortcut is shorter," Nick said.

"That's the way Jake went home when he was bit by the bat..." my voice trailed off.

"Are you going chicken on me?" Nick said.

I swallowed hard. "Come on Nick, you're not going to go that way."

"Just watch me," he stepped into the vacant lot and made his way to the forest. He paused at the edge, "Coming?"

I stood my ground.

"Well, I'll meet you there." He stepped into the brush and was gone.

Which way should I go? It would take me a lot longer to go around the blocks. "Nick, wait up," I called. "Nick!" I ran after him and entered the woods. The darkness and coolness swallowed me. I took a few steps and paused. "Nick, where are you?"

A hand touched my shoulder, and I dropped Jake's bag. I spun around and looked at Nick. "Thanks," I said.

"I knew you'd come this way. It's faster." Little did he know how fast it would be.

We had walked for about fifty feet, when we heard it. It was soft at first, but grew in speed and intensity.

"Do you hear that?"

Flap, flap.

It was getting louder and closer.

I turned to look over my shoulder and saw something black fly over my head.

It swooped around my head and then flew toward Nick.

"Duck," I shouted.

Nick hit the dirt and then I saw what it was, a bat, a big, black bat.

A vampire bat.

The bat circled back and headed for Nick who was sprawled on the ground.

I ripped the backpack from my back and swung it high. The bag connected with the bat.

A high-pitched squeal and fluttering sounded on the other side of the bag.

I brought the backpack down and saw the bat hanging on to the other side. "He won't let go." I shook the bag as hard as I could, but it clung to the straps for all its worth.

The black body flopped over and moved closer to my hand, but I wouldn't let it have Jake's backpack.

I swung it toward a tree, and the impact stunned me.

The bat dropped to the ground, flapped around, and then flew up and away from us.

Nick scrambled to his feet, grabbed the other strap on Jake's bag and pulled me through the woods.

Nick and I burst out of the woods and entered Jake's backyard. We fell on the ground, panting frantically, trying to catch our breath.

Nick rolled over, and I looked into my eyes. "Were you bit?" I asked.

"No, were you?" Nick felt his neck and looked at me.

"No," I said, as a big gasp of air exited my lungs. I looked into Jake's house as we tried to regroup. The curtains were open in his dining room. A huge mirror ran the length of the wall. We loved playing cards in that room. Few people ever thought to worry if we could see their cards in that mirror.

"Isn't it funny how no one ever thinks about that mirror when we play cards?" Nick said.

"I was just thinking about that."

Jake walked through the dining room and passed by the window.

"Look, there's Jake now," Nick said.

But my eyes couldn't believe what they were seeing. "Oh no. Look."

"What? I see Jake. What's the problem?" Nick asked.

I pointed and said, "Look into the mirror."

Then Nick saw what I had seen. Jake wasn't casting a reflection in the mirror.

Jake was a vampire.

Jake answered the door. His neck was still wrapped in gauze and his eyes looked sunken in his head. "Wait until you see my new digs."

"What?" I said.

"My surprise. I have a new room. If I would have known all I had to do was to get bit by a bat to get a new room, I would have thought of that long ago."

Nick and I headed to the stairs going up to the second floor.

Jack shook his head. "Not upstairs, I'm downstairs in the crypt."

I tried not to react.

"My room is soo cool and soo quiet."

We followed him through the kitchen and went down the stairs into the basement. "It's dark, and I'll sleep like the dead down here."

"Why did your parents move you down here?" I asked.

"My parents said I'd like it better down here."

"Did they say why?" Nick asked.

"I'd have more room and privacy down here."

CHapter Five

The next week passed quickly, and Jake didn't return to school. I had tried to call him, but no one ever answered the phone. At least, no one answered during the day, and I didn't try after sunset.

Just as our math test was finishing up, a knock came on the classroom door. A man entered carrying a box. He set it down on Mrs. Hubers' desk and left.

Mrs. Hubers opened the box and looked inside. "Your class pictures came back already." Mrs. Hubers touched the box on her desk.

The class erupted in chatter.

"Mom said she was going to use my picture for our Christmas card," Nick moaned. "I hope it's not lame."

"Ryan and I refuse to be mailed to anyone." Matthew leaned forward to see if he could peek into the box.

Mrs. Hubers realized her mistake. "All right, I'll pass them out now, but you'll have to keep them in your desk, so they don't get bent. Your parents will be upset if they come home with wrinkles. So promise me, you'll keep them safe."

"We promise," the class said together.

"Okay, once you get your pictures, you can run to the restroom. When you get back, take out your notebooks and finish your essays." She pulled out one envelope. "Matthew," she called.

I stood up and walked to her desk. "Thank you," I said, as she handed me the packet. A clear window revealed a picture of me looking out. My smile looked dorky, my blond hair stuck straight up, and I didn't want to give them to Mom. I slipped them into my desk and headed out the door.

"Nick," Mrs. Hubers called.

I took a long drink at the water fountain as I waited for Nick.

He came out of the classroom with his head hanging.

"I hate my picture too," I said.

Nick exhaled and shook his head.

"I'm sure it's not that bad," I said.

Our classmate Jane Thomas came out of our classroom. She looked at us and walked to the girl's room.

"Looks like we're not the only ones," Nick said. Then a smile played across his mouth. "I wonder how Jake's picture turned out." He put his hand on his neck. "I bet all we can see is that bandage. I wish I had a bandage to cover my whole face."

"Me too, one that covers everything," I added.

"I wonder what Jake's looked like," Nick said.

Mrs. Hubers walked out of the room and headed down the hall.

"We should go check them out." Nick motioned for me to follow. He hurried back into our classroom.

I followed close behind.

Mrs. Hubers had passed out all of the pictures before our afternoon bathroom break, so Jake's must have been in his desk. We stood in the doorway and watched as the rest of our classmates headed to the restroom.

Nick grabbed my arm. "When we get done with lunch,

we'll sneak back early and look at Jake's pictures."

Mrs. Hubers stood behind us. "Are you guys going in? You have work to do."

Nick smiled. "We're on our way." He quickly slipped into his desk and pulled his notebook out. He carefully avoided looking at his pictures.

I smiled as I opened my desk. Quickly, I turned my pictures over and took my notebook out.

Nick leaned over and said, "Lunchtime," and gave me the thumbs up.

Nick shoveled his food in like he was starving. "Hurry up, Matthew. I want to get back to see...I mean get to my...my report."

I took the last bite of my peanut butter sandwich and wiped my hands on my pants.

"Ready," I said. Throwing my garbage away, I followed Nick out of the cafeteria and back to our classroom.

"What if Mrs. Hubers comes back early/" I asked.

"We'll tell her we're going to bring Jake's homework to him."

We moved over to Jake's desk and opened it. "I don't think we should do this," I said, stopping Nick from turning over the envelope.

"That's for sure."

Both Nick and I turned around and saw Little Cody standing in the doorway.

"Spying on your little friend? What will you guys do next?" Little Cody walked over to join us at Jake's desk.

My face burned red as Nick's shoe tried to dig into

the floor.

"Well, let's see it," Little Cody said. "You've gone this far."

Nick reached in and flipped the envelope over.

The three of us gasped at the same time. Mrs. Hubers' name was written on the dry erase board. The board sat on the stool, but one thing was missing.

"Where's Jake?" Nick asked. He opened the envelope and pulled the pictures out. They were all the same. A dry erase board sat on a stool, but no Jake.

Little Cody backed away from the desk and us. "Vampires can't be caught on film. Your friend is a vampire," he said. "And if you're not careful, you two will be too." He turned and fled from the room.

CHapter Six

"Matthew, telephone," Mom called.

"I'll get it up here," I called down the steps. "Hello," I said, as I brought the phone to my ear.

"Matthew, how's it going?" Jake's voice was like it always had been, happy.

That's when panic struck. Wasn't that the trick of the vampire? Make you believe all is well and good, and then they bite you on the neck.

"Oh, hi," I said.

"I wanted to thank you for picking up my homework. My mom baked some chocolate chip cookies for you and Nick. I was hoping to drop them off tonight when I picked up my homework, if that's okay?"

"Sure," I said and paused, as Mom walked up the stairs.

"Is Nick coming over for supper tonight?" she asked.

I nodded.

"Why don't you invite Jake over too?" Mom asked.

I shook my head, but Jake must have heard her offer.

"That would be fun, just like old times," Jake said. "I'll ask my mom to bring me over earlier, I'm sure she won't mind."

My heart sank. My mom invited the vampire over to our house. Vampires can't enter your home unless you invite them in, and Mom just invited him in.

I called Nick as soon as I hung up the phone with Jake.

"Vampires can't come in, unless they are invited in," Nick said.

"I know, so, if we open the door and step back, but don't invite Jake in, we can prove he's a vampire?"

"Exactly," Nick said.

"But does Mom's invite count?"

"I think it has to be at the door, when he is invited in then and there." Nick didn't sound so sure of his answer.

"Well, we have a plan, as long as nothing goes wrong." I crossed my fingers.

"What could possibly go wrong?" Nick asked.

Why did those words stab fear into my heart?

The doorbell rang. Nick and I raced to the door and opened it.

Jake held up two bags of warm cookies. He turned around and waved to his mom.

She drove away.

"We'll see if Jake can enter the house without our invite," Nick whispered.

"Come on in, Jake," Ryan said, as he pushed between us leaving the house. "I'm heading to the movies, so save some supper for me." And he was gone.

I looked at Nick as Jake entered the house and shook my head. Both my mother and my brother had foiled our plan.

Nick came out of the kitchen smiling. He winked at me as he found his chair across the table from me. "Plan B," he whispered.

Before I could ask what Plan B was, Mom called from the kitchen. "Matthew, can you help me in here?"

"I'll be right in," I said.

Jake finished setting the table and sat down next to me.

"I'll be right back." I inhaled deeply as I entered the kitchen. Roast beef and Mom's famous garlic mashed potatoes...

Garlic mashed potatoes...

An idea popped into my mind. As I neared the stove, I said, "Mom, can we dish out the food on the plates, before we bring them out?"

Mom turned from the sink and looked at me. "Sure, I guess we could, but wouldn't it be easier to..."

"In school today, we learned about the maids and butlers in England serving food, so I thought we could try that."

Mom smiled. "I think that would be fun." She set the dinner plates on the counter and started scooping out mashed potatoes. "Could you get the butter out of the refrigerator?"

I opened the refrigerator's door. The small bottle of mashed garlic sat on the door's shelf. I slipped it into my pocket and took the butter to Mom.

"We need to wear aprons, don't we?"

"I have the perfect one, I'll be right back," Mom said.

As Mom left the room, I opened the garlic and spooned some into the potatoes on Jake's plate. I mixed it up and slipped the bottle back.

"Are we ready?" Mom finished tying her apron and picked up two plates.

"I have Jake and my plate here," I said.

"Then this is Nick's and mine," she said. She pushed the swinging door out of our way, and we entered the dining room. "Dinner is served."

I placed Jake's plate down in front of him.

"Everything smells so good," Jake said.

"My Mom's a great cook," I said proudly.

Nick took a big spoonful of mashed potatoes and shoved them into his mouth. "Mmmm, these are the best potatoes in the world," Nick said, with his mouthful.

Jake took a scoop of potatoes and smelled them. He took a big bite and held them in his mouth. His eyes widened, and he gasped. Potatoes burst out of his mouth and across his plate.

Nick, Mom and I looked on in horror.

"Jake, were those potatoes too hot?" Mom worried about her recipe as Jake spit the rest of the potatoes out.

But Nick and I knew that Jake was a vampire.

CHapter Seven

Saturday raced by with all of the chores Mom and Dad had planned. Raking leaves and trimming plants for winter wasn't what I had planned to do, but Mom bribed Ryan and me with pizza, and Dad promised triple allowances.

What could Ryan and I do?

Chief ran through the piles of leaves and around the backyard. He played fetch with the sticks and chased the rabbits and squirrels, but did little to help. He only entertained us.

During a quick break, Nick signaled to me from his bedroom window that he'd stop over after supper.

Mom joined me. She looked up to Nick's window. "What are you two scheming?"

"No-nothing," I lied.

"Invite Nick over for pizza, I'm sure there will be enough Angelo's Pizza." She smiled and returned to bagging leaves.

Before supper, Nick slipped a book out from underneath his jacket. "I hope this can help us." He placed the book on my bed. *The Complete Book of Vampire* was worn and leather bound.

"Dad had this on his shelf. I can't believe he had something like this," Nick said.

I quickly flipped to the bookmarked place. "How to Kill a Vampire" was the title of the chapter.

Nick pointed at the list. "Wooden stakes, garlic, holy

water, crosses, and fire."

"But we want him to cure him, not kill him."

Nick looked at me as if I had two heads as he handed me a small glass bottle. "It's holy water. My Grandma Georgia gave it to me. She told me it was to keep vampires away, but I know she gave it to me to keep me safe. She's like that you know."

"You have a strange family, but then again, mine is weird too."

"Takes one to know one," he said, as I took the small bottle and put it on my bookshelf.

"My mom has a whole wreath of garlic," Nick said.

"She does? Talk about strange." I sniffed a few times. "Now, I know why you smell like that."

Nick pushed me down on the floor and put me in a headlock.

"Careful. I don't want the bottle to fall off the shelf." I warned, through clenched teeth.

Nick let go. "Sorry." He stood up and headed to the door. "I'll run home and get a few crosses, the garlic, and the wooden tent stakes."

"Run fast, before the pizza gets here."

Nick ran down the back stairs, and I watched from my window as he entered his house. A few minutes later, he emerged with his backpack.

He entered my room and threw the items on the bed. "All we need is fire." Nick carefully placed the holy water into the bag.

"We have a grill lighter that we could use. I'll grab

that after supper."

"Matthew, Nick, supper," my mom called.

Nick and I raced each other to the table.

After supper, I asked, "Mom, can we work on the computer for a while?"

"Is it for a school project?" she asked as she continued washing the dishes.

"Preventing Jake from turning into a vampire is the most important project we have at school," Nick whispered to me.

"Yes, it's a big project, very important." I pleaded with my eyes. "Nick can help me, and we'll be done even faster."

"You can use it for half an hour, but no games."

"Thanks, Mom." I rushed to the computer and turned it on.

"What are you hoping we'll find?" Nick asked.

The internet came on, and I Googled, "How do you prevent a friend from turning into a vampire?"

Several websites came up.

"Try that one," Nick said, pointing to "Vampirepedia. com".

"How to make a vampire, how to avoid a vampire attack, what vampires eat...how to prevent becoming a vampire." Nick and I read the heading at the same time.

"There," Nick pointed.

I brought the cursor to the heading and clicked.

"Vampires hate garlic, holy water, wooden stakes,

roses, crosses and bells."

"Bells?" we said at the same time.

"All of these items will keep vampires away."

"I have an idea. If we put the garlic into the holy water…" I started.

"And we made Jake wear crosses and bells…"

"We could prevent him from turning into a vampire."

"Exactly."

"Wooden stakes, fire and decapitation will kill a vampire," I read out loud.

"Remember, we want to cure him, not kill him."

"What if we can't prevent him from becoming a vampire?" I asked.

"That's not an option," Nick said.

After Mom finished in the kitchen, we snuck in to fill Grandma Georgia's bottle of holy water with the mashed garlic from the refrigerator. I shook it well and watched as the mixture spun. Hopefully, the two combined together would be strong enough to prevent Jake from turning into a full-blooded vampire.

"I've seen every episode of Buffy the Vampire Slayer and Angel," Nick said. "I think we're ready."

I had seen all of the shows too, but I doubted that they would get us ready for this battle. Crosses, strings of bells, holy water, and cloves of garlic were carefully packed into Nick's backpack.

Looking at all the prevention weapons collected in the bag, I wondered. Would any of these things work on Jake? He was my friend, and I didn't want him to be a vampire. Could we turn him back into a human?

We would soon find out.

CHapter Eight

It was Saturday night, and Ryan offered to give us a ride over to Jake's house. He pulled over at Jake's corner. Ryan unbuckled his seatbelt and took out his wallet. He fished out a twenty dollar bill. "If you need a ride home, you can always call a cab, if you can't get a ride from Jake's dad. Dad's bowling tonight, so he won't be home." Ryan looked at them and squinted. "Does Jake even know you guys are coming over?"

Nick and I said nothing.

Ryan nodded at us and gave me a questioning look.

"Ryan, we're fine, we'll figure it out," I said.

He pushed the money into my hand. "Take it. You can always pay me back."

I took the money and slipped it into my pocket. "Okay, but I owe you."

"Okay," Ryan said.

Nick and I stood on the curb. "Don't forget to hook your seatbelt," I said.

"Yes, Mom," he said and laughed, but didn't fasten it. He drove off into the night.

"Are you ready?" Nick asked.

"I guess," I said, as we started toward Jake's house. This time, Ryan dropped us across the street from Jake's house, so we didn't have to take the short cut. Thank goodness.

"Should we go into the house or lure him outside?" Nick asked.

We crossed the street to Jake's house and paused. As we watched, Jake walked by the front window. We could hear Jake's voice from outside.

"Mom, have you seen my skateboard?" he called.

"Why is he looking for his skateboard this late at night?" Nick asked.

"I don't know. It is pretty late to be boarding." I looked at the rapidly approaching night.

"No, Mom. I'm not going to Dead Man's Drop," Jake shouted back into the house as he burst out the front door.

We jumped back behind the shrubs as he flew down the steps. He jumped on his skateboard and rolled down the sidewalk.

"Let's follow him," Nick said.

"Right behind you." We barely kept up with him.

Jake kicked the ground and sent his skateboard rolling faster. He sailed down the sidewalk. He turned the corner and headed toward the skateboard park. His hair flew along the side of his head. It looked like wings, flapping in the night breeze.

"Where's he going?" Nick asked.

"He mentioned Dead Man's Drop, but no one has ever made that jump. He'll kill himself." I said, as we raced after him.

We cut through the block and took positions behind the hedge that surrounded the park.

Jake skated down the snaking trail and did a ring around the bowl at the far side of the park. When he headed in our direction, we ducked. He circled the loop and took a second pass.

We moved down to Dead Man's Drop and waited.

Jake rode high on one of the sides of the snake, the large S-shaped run in the skateboard park. It looked like he was trying to gain speed as he prepared to try Dead Man's Drop.

"He won't make it," Nick said, from between clenched teeth.

"He'll kill himself," I said.

"But he's a vampire. Isn't he part of the living dead?" Nick asked.

Jake skimmed along the rim and suddenly veered to the jump. He crouched low to cut wind resistance and aimed straight and true. He whizzed behind a tree. There was a rustle in the leaves and his skateboard shot off the ramp and into the night.

But Jake was gone!

Replaced above the skateboard was a big black bat. He flew above the skateboard and straight up into the air. He swirled around the streetlamp, did a figure eight, and returned back to the old oak tree.

Leaves rustled again and Jake stepped out from behind the tree. He gave a great whoop and ran after his skateboard. His hair flew in the breeze. He seemed to float in mid-air as he headed home.

Chapter Nine

"Let's head him off before he gets home," Nick said.

I grabbed Nick's backpack, and we raced through the skateboard park.

In the wooded area a block away from Jake's house, we hid in the bushes. The rasping roll of wheels on the sidewalk alerted us that he was close.

"You hit him high, and I'll hit him low, and we'll roll him into the woods and make him drink the holy water and dress him in bells and crosses." Nick hunched low and waved me into action.

Jake's wheels neared, and my body tensed.

"Now!" Nick yelled.

We jumped out of the bushes and landed directly in Jake's path. I raised my arms and reached for Jake's shoulders. Nick squatted down and dove for his legs. Both of our bodies hit him at the same time, and the three of us rolled into the woods, as his skateboard continued on down the sidewalk.

Nick rolled over on top of Jake and held him to the ground. "Now, Matthew, now."

I ripped open the backpack and pulled the bottle of holy water out. My fingers frantically uncorked it, and I stepped over his head.

"What's in there?" Jake asked when he saw the bottle.

I poured the holy water onto Jake's mouth and backed up. "Garlic and holy water. We're trying to prevent you from turning into a vampire."

Jake yelled and coughed as he spit and sputtered.

I closed my eyes, not wanting to see Jake's skin blister and burn. I couldn't bear to see his face peel off, or hear his screams of pain.

But Jake wasn't screaming.

I peeked out from between my eyelids. Jake's wet face looked at Nick, trying to figure out what was going on.

Nick's face was turned away from us, his body tense and ready.

I reached over and touched Nick's arm.

"Is he dead?" Nick asked.

"No, he's fine," Jake said.

Nick looked down at Jake. "He's talking. Should we try the crosses and bells?"

I stared at him. "If the holy water didn't work, why would they work?'

"Come on guys, you really think I'm a vampire?" Jake asked. He pushed on Nick. "Please, let me up."

"How do we know that you're not a vampire?" Nick asked.

Jake pushed Nick away from him and sat up. "Vampires don't say please." He wiped his face off with his sleeve. "So, you guys thought I was a vampire. What ever made you think that?"

"You were bit by a bat," I reminded him.

"And your eyes hurt in the sun," Nick added.

"I had pink eye," he said.

"You were hot and cold," I said.

"I had a slight reaction to the rabies vaccine," Jake

said.

"Your parents moved you into the basement." Nick pointed out.

"My mother is pregnant, and they wanted my room for the nursery."

Nick sat back and scratched his head. "You didn't cast a reflection in the mirror."

"When?" Jake asked.

"The first night we dropped your homework off," I said.

"Our dining room mirror?" Jake asked. He fell back on the ground and laughed. "My parents are remodeling the dining room, and when they took the mirror down, the backing came off. All that was left was the glass. No mirror action."

"So you say," Nick said. "What about the potatoes?"

"The potatoes?" Jake asked. "Oh, the mashed potatoes? They were so strong, I couldn't swallow them. Matthew, your mom uses way too much garlic when she cooks."

Nick's face flushed. "Oops," he said.

"What do you mean by oops?" I asked.

"I kind of added some garlic to your mom's mashed potatoes. I wanted to see if Jake would react to garlic, so I added more to the mashed potatoes."

Now it was my turn for my face to burn. "Oops. I added garlic to your mashed potatoes too," I said.

Jake and Nick turned to me. "You didn't," Jake said.

I nodded. "I did. I added garlic to your potatoes before I served them to you."

"No wonder he couldn't breathe after one mouthful," Nick said.

"You guys tried to kill me with garlic," Jake said.

"Okay, but what about your school pictures?" Nick demanded. "Your smiling face wasn't in any of them."

"My mom called Mrs. Hubers the day of the school pictures and asked her to tell the photographer not to use the pictures he took of me. She didn't want the bandage to be in the picture, so she hoped that I would be able to have a make up session."

"Okay, we can give you that, but we just saw you turn into a bat. You can't deny that."

"I didn't turn into a bat." Jake shook his head.

I nodded. "Down at Dead Man's Drop. We saw you turn into a bat. You flew up and over the streetlight, just now. We saw it."

"I didn't turn into a bat." Jake picked up his skateboard and shook it. "I rode Dead Man's Drop, but I'm not stupid enough to try and jump it. I'd kill myself."

"I know what I saw," Nick said.

"I swung up into the tree just before I went off the jump. There's a low branch that I grabbed onto and pulled myself into the tree. When I entered the branches, I scared a big bat out of the tree. It flew over my skateboard and around the light, just as you said, but it wasn't me. It came back and scared me out of the tree. After his first bite, I wasn't going to let him do that again. So I jumped out of the tree and picked up my skateboard. That's when you guys decided to drown me in garlic water, and here we are."

Before anyone could say a word, a pair of headlights

swung through the woods.

"It's the cops," Nick said. "Let's get out of here."

The three of us froze in our spots, afraid of being found.

The headlights swung around again and aimed directly at us. The lights flashed to high beams and pinned us to our spot.

Chapter Ten

The headlights pulled up closer and blinded us.

"Matthew, is that you?" my Dad's voice demanded, as he opened the door.

"Yeah," I said, weakly.

"Get in the car, now. We have to get you to the hospital." Dad slipped back inside and closed the car door.

"But Dad..." I started.

"Just get in the car. Hurry." Dad was upset and sounded like he was going to cry.

I wiped my hands on my pants and ran to the car. Didn't he know that Jake wasn't a vampire, and he didn't have rabies? He had pink eye, and a reaction to his shots.

I didn't want to get a shot for anything.

"Jake, don't forget your skateboard. I'll see you guys tomorrow," I called back to Nick and Jake, but wondered if that was true.

Dad beeped the horn to hurry me along.

I jumped into the car and quickly fastened my seatbelt.

Dad pulled away from the curb, squealing the tires as we left.

Dad drove in silence, staring straight ahead.

What was wrong? Did I do something bad? Why were we going to the hospital? Mom didn't get off work until late tonight.

Dad pulled the car into the emergency room parking

lot and jumped out.

I hurried to keep up with him. We never parked here before. We always parked in the ramp. Why wasn't Dad talking to me?

Dad paused at the elevator. The doors opened, and we stepped inside. He pushed the "three" button. Mom worked on the fifth floor.

Before I could ask if he pushed the wrong button, the doors opened and Dad stepped out.

Dad rushed down the hallway and through a set of double doors. The big letters of ICU were above the doors. He walked past the nurse's station and entered a room.

I caught up and stopped in the doorway. Mom stood by the bed with red eyes and a Kleenex in her hand. She stepped back.

Two white casts covered the person's legs. IV tubes ran into both arms. I looked up to the head of the bed. A metal frame was screwed into the skull of the patient. Then I recognized the person lying in the bed, after all, he was my brother.

"Ryan was in a car accident. A car hit him on his way home from his friend's house. He broke both legs and a bone in his neck, that's why he has that halo to stabilize his spine."

"Hey Matthew," Ryan slurred. "Come closer."

I took a tentative step.

"I can't turn my head, but I'm sure I look like one of your movie monsters." His arm made a jerky, uncoordinated motion in my direction.

I jumped back.

Dad continued, "Ryan will be fine. He's just all banged up. We're going to need your help at home while he..."

But my mind was screaming,

OH NO, MY BROTHER IS
FRANKENSTEIN'S MONSTER!

Author's Bio

LANCE ZARIMBA lives in a haunted house that man who invented Old Dutch potato chips built. He works as an occupational therapist in Minneapolis, MN. He helps people with hand and finger injuries. It is only natural, that he grew up watching *Dark Shadows* in the Upper Peninsula of Michigan and enjoys all of the classic monster movies. He has read every Hardy Boys and Nancy Drew book. His nephew, Matthew, helped him come up with the idea of *Oh No, My Best Friend is a Zombie* and *Oh No, Our Best Friend is a Vampire*. Lance is currently working on the third book in the series, *Oh No, My Brother is Frankenstein's Monster*. His house is full of books, and his white schnauzer, Ripley, who helps him write his stories. He can be reached at LanceZarimba@ yahoo.com.

9 781608 202225